To Hilda
I hope you
enjoy reading to your
grandchildren Love E

the adventures of
Ana the bee

WRITTEN BY
evelyn sanchez-toledo

ILLUSTRATED BY JESÚS GALLARDO

Illustrated by Jesús Gallardo

ISBN: 978-1-957058-18-4
Library of Congress Control Number: 2021919536

FIG
FACTOR
MEDIA

Dedication

I dedicate this book to the children, lovers of nature and its wonders. May the buzzing of bees remind you of all the beauty and good they create.

Acknowledgements

I would like to thank my friends and family for their support and encouragement during my journey writing this book. Thank you to Jackie Camacho for her insight. Special thanks to my kids, Samuel, Daniella, Alexis, Katie, Mariela, Ricky, and my sister Aida, who may not always understand my crazy but always support and love me.

Introduction

Where there are flowers, there are bees. There are over 20,000 species of bees and over 250,000 recorded flowering plants. Bees can be found on every continent except Antarctica. Bees help pollinate flowers and many crops. They are the only insect that provide a product that can be consumed by humans, honey.* If the bees die off, so will many flowers. They rely on each other. We rely on them. Let's protect them both.

The idea for this book came to me as a dream during this historical time of pandemics. It was a reminder to cherish the good and the beauty in nature. What better way to do this than through *the Adventures of Ana the bee.*

*More information about bees can be found on https://www.usgs.gov/faqs/how-many-species-native-bees-are-united-states

More information about flowers on https://sciencetrends.com/types-of-flowers-list-and-names/

Ana is a curious little worker bee that likes adventures. She wanted to travel and explore the city and countryside. One day she decided to hide in a box of **lilies** and **poppies**. That's where her adventure began.

She was searching for the most beautiful flowers. White **begonias** were the first flowers Ana saw. They were drenched with water on a boat, but she couldn't get near them because there were some hungry flies nearby. *How frightening!* Those flies eat bees. Scared, Ana returned to her hive.

6

In the evening, she left her hive to eat *pumpkin flowers* and she saw a centipede. It came out every evening at the same time to eat from the *bluebell flowers* and the *leaves of the carnations*. Since the centipede didn't pay her any attention, Ana was able to eat peacefully.

As she listened to the sounds of the cicadas, Ana hid in the chimney inside a hut. No one could see her, but she was worried. A fire could be started and the smoke would make her fall asleep.

In front of the hut, Ana saw a row of *dahlias* of various colors. She decided to count them. There were twelve! She liked those the best because they were sweet and delicious. Ana ate from the flowers and went on her way until it started to get dark.

10

With the light of the moon, Ana entered a house and saw a **star of Bethlehem plant** in an elegant pot. She hid quickly, because a lady appeared with a broom to shoo her away. Oh, no!

When the sun came out, Ana flew to a field of flowers. At the end of the field there was a flaming ***flamboyan tree***. There, she was able to hide and easily enjoy the day.

She continued her travels until, tired, she sat under the shade of a large ***sunflower***. Ana observed how worms enjoyed the seeds that covered the ground. She also enjoyed the perfume of the ***gardenias*** that were nearby.

13

It was very hot, so Ana stopped to drink water from a can that was near some beautiful *hydrangeas*. While she enjoyed the flowers, Ana noticed a spider 's web. Be careful not to fall in!

15

Later that day, Ana decided to go to an island near the lake to see her bee friend. She showed Ana flowers named *irises*. They were so beautiful! Afterwards, the friends flew to an immense garden across the way.

The friends were attracted to the *jasmines* because of their fragrance. Nearby, there was a tree with juicy mangos, on which several birds were playing. Ana was afraid of the birds and decided not to stop. Her friend said goodbye and returned to the island.

While she was flying, Ana saw her friend Kique, a butterfly who lived near the home of Kikiriki the rooster. Upon reuniting, together, they did somersaults in the air.

Suddenly it started to rain, and Ana and Kique quietly stayed contemplating the *lilies* that adorned the house. It was raining too hard to go out!

When the rain stopped, they went to visit a hill filled with many flowers. Together with the butterfly, Ana shared the delicacies of the **daisies** to create the sticky honey.

Ana had never seen **daffodils**. She didn't realize that she was sitting amongst them, and no one around had noticed her. How mischievous! Kique the butterfly decided to stay, and Ana continued her trip.

Ana flew through a vegetable garden and found that she disliked the large leaves of the yams, so she continued until she saw a group of children playing. The children saw her and started fanning their arms like crazy so she would leave.

What a scare!

24

Soon she arrived at the market. Ana had only seen *orchids* in the store. There were eight in beautiful pots. She also found a caterpillar with small eyes — our little bee decided to sit near it to rest until the next day.

In the Morning, in the garden of a small house in town, Ana found a group of bees by the purple and white *petunias*. Suddenly, the bees started to bother Ana because she was from another hive. Sadly, Ana had to leave.

She had a long way to go to reach her final destination. *How far could it be?* She flew in the direction of a light in the distance. When she arrived, she saw it was an electric bug zapper! Luckily, Ana didn't get close.

Next Morning, Ana felt the sprinkling of water that fell on the *roses* which decorated a round cart where she was resting. The roses were of rare and radiant colors. All of a sudden, she felt things move. Someone had purchased the bouquet of roses she was in. Ana flew away quickly.

Nearby, there were *sage plants* that grew between the sun and the shade. Ana loved the taste of the flowers. After enjoying them, she took flight and continued her travels.

Ana passed where the *tulips* grow in the spring. There were many of different sizes and colors.

She also flew by a *vineyard*. The small green flowers of the grapes were blooming. *The flowers are so small—they are the size of a human fingernail!*

Ana then went to where the *violets* were. That day, many bees had come from all over to see the variety of colors.

36

As night fell, a *wisteria* vine that covered the gate became a good hiding place for Ana to rest. At sunrise, she went on her way.

She arrived at Señora Xiomara's home and stood on a *xanadu* plant that was flowering. Ana couldn't stay there because she noticed Señora Xiomara used pesticides. Oh, no! That was poisonous for a little bee.

Several hours had passed when she arrived at her very own garden. In between the weeds, she noticed a *yucca plant* that also had flowers. Ana was happy, as she was nearing her destination.

As she flew by the zinnias, Ana heard her family buzzing energetically. She arrived at her hive that was beyond the tall *grass*. Ana, the little worker bee, was happy to be home and ready to tell them about her adventures and all the flowers she had seen.

 **THE END**

About Evelyn Sanchez-Toledo

Born in Arecibo, Puerto Rico, raised in Chicago's Humboldt Park Community, I graduated from Northeastern Illinois University. I am a mother of 3, and a grandmother. As a retired dual language teacher, I have decided to dedicate myself to writing. My children's books are inspired by my grandchildren, the world around them and nature. My previous books are Diego's New America and Bruna Dancing Around the World.

Made in the USA
Middletown, DE
20 February 2022